D0624594

Aurora's Story

Adapted by Courtney Carbone

Illustrated by the Disney Storybook Art Team

A Random House PICTUREBACK® Book
Random House New York

Copyright © 2019 Disney Enterprises, Inc. All rights reserved. Published in the United States by Random House Children's Books, a division of Penguin Random House LLC, 1745 Broadway, New York, NY 10019, and in Canada by Penguin Random House Canada Limited, Toronto, in conjunction with Disney Enterprises, Inc. Pictureback, Random House, and the Random House colophon are registered trademarks of Penguin Random House LLC.
rhcbooks.com
ISBN 978-0-7364-4058-5
Printed in the United States of America
10 9 8 7 6 5 4 3 2 1

Hello! I am PRINCESS AURORA. My name means "dawn." I have three magical fairy godmothers named FLORA, FAUNA, and MERRYWEATHER.

My parents, the King and Queen, dreamed of having a baby for a long time. When I was born, there was a huge celebration at the castle.

An evil fairy named MALEFICENT showed up uninvited—and put a terrible curse on me!

Merryweather tried to help, but Maleficent's spell was too strong.
It became destined that on my sixteenth birthday, I would prick my
finger on the spindle of a spinning wheel and fall into a deep sleep.

My father ordered all of the spinning wheels in the entire kingdom be destroyed.

Still, my parents worried that it wasn't enough.
The fairies came up with a plan to keep me safe
from Maleficent. They would hide me in a cottage
deep in the woods until my sixteenth birthday.

Maleficent wasn't giving up that easily. From high in her castle on the Forbidden Mountain, she ordered her raven to find out where I was hiding. The wicked bird searched the kingdom high and low for years and years.

As time passed, I grew into a young woman. My godmothers took good care of me. They gave me the name BRIAR ROSE so I wouldn't know the truth about my past. I never would have guessed I was really a princess!

I dreamed of meeting someone special. Finally, on my sixteenth birthday, I met a handsome prince named PHILLIP while out in the woods. We fell in love as we danced and sang together. It was a dream come true!

When I told my godmothers
I had met someone special, they
grew very worried.

They told me the truth about who I was
and rushed me back home to the castle. I thought
I would never see Phillip again.

My whole life changed in just one day. I wanted to spend time with Phillip, but instead I was far away and very lonely.

It turned out I wasn't alone— Maleficent had found me!

The fearsome fairy placed me under a spell. I followed
her to a hidden room, where a spinning wheel was waiting.
I couldn't stop myself from touching the spindle.

Maleficent cackled with glee. Her curse came true! I fell into a deep sleep.

While I slumbered, Flora gave
Phillip an enchanted sword and
shield to fight Maleficent.

Furious, the evil fairy turned into a fierce, fire-breathing dragon! Phillip fought bravely, and at just the right moment, he threw his sword. Maleficent stumbled forward—and fell off a steep cliff!

With Maleficent defeated, Phillip ran to my side.
He knew that the only thing that could break the
spell was a kiss from my true love.

When Phillip kissed me, the curse was broken. I awoke from my deep sleep.

The entire kingdom rejoiced when they learned I was safe and sound.
I rushed into the arms of my parents. We were finally reunited! I was very
happy to be back with my family and take my rightful place as the Princess.

Now I look forward to my new life and a future of happiness
with all the people I love. I am free to create my own destiny!